Nobody Likes To Lose

Words by Lydia Marshall

Pictures by Eric Oxendorf

 CHILDRENS PRESS, CHICAGO

3 4 5 6 7 8 9 10 11 12 R 86 85 84 83 82

Library of Congress Cataloging in Publication Data

Marshall, Lydia.
  Nobody likes to lose.

  SUMMARY: Sandy comes in last in her heat at the
swim meet but learns the difference between winning
against herself and winning against others.
  [1. Swimming—Fiction.   2. Winning and losing—
Fiction] I. Oxendorf, Eric. II. Title.
PZ7.M356725No   [E]   79-22359
ISBN 0-516-01478-1

Nobody Likes To Lose

Sandy stood near the pool, wiggling her arms and shaking one leg and then the other. With all the noise, she couldn't hear her mom and dad. But she knew they were sitting on one side of the swimming pool and cheering for her. She could see her coach, kneeling near the edge of the pool. She knew he would be shouting, "Move it, Sandy." And she knew her best friend, Emily, would be yelling, "Let's go, Sandy."

But all of it wasn't going to do her any good, she thought. The other girls she was racing against would beat her. She would lose again.

Above the noise came a voice over the loudspeaker: "The next event is the 25-yard freestyle for girls eight and under." Sandy pulled at her yellow bathing cap to make it tighter. She took a few deep breaths. Then the starter, who was standing at the side of the pool, said, "Swimmers, take your marks!" In his hand was a small pistol, and his finger was on the trigger.

Sandy curled her toes over the edge of the pool. Then she bent forward so that her fingers gripped the edge just outside her toes.

"Here goes nothing," Sandy said to herself as the gun went bang. When she hit the water, she began kicking her feet and pulling with her arms as fast as she could. She tried to keep her head in the water and not to turn it to breathe too often. That would slow her down.

As soon as she touched the wall at the other end of the pool she looked around. All the other girls had finished before her. Even though her time was the fastest she had ever done, she had lost again.

She dragged herself out of the pool. With her head down and her shoulders slumped, she walked slowly to a corner.

The kids on her team, the Rosedale Sharks, were resting between races. They had stretched out towels and were sitting on them. As Sandy plopped down on her towel, Emily smiled and said, "Good going, Sandy."

"Good going?" Sandy grunted. "I was last as usual."

"Never mind that," said Emily. "You bettered your time. That's all that matters. You're only seven years old. You can't expect to beat girls who are going on nine. You . . ."

Before Emily could finish, another announcement came over the loudspeaker: "The next event will be the 50-yard freestyle for nine- and ten-year-old girls."

"I'll see you later, Sandy," Emily said. She trotted off as Sandy grumbled something after her. She should have wished Emily luck, but Emily didn't need any luck. She had won dozens of ribbons and medals. And at four meets she had won trophies for being the best eight and under girl swimmer. Emily's father had just built a shelf in her room on which he put all her prizes.

But now, Sandy thought, maybe things were going to be a little different. Emily would be racing against girls who might be almost two years older than she was. Maybe now she would learn what it felt like to lose. Sandy didn't even bother to get up from her towel to watch Emily swim and cheer her on.

In a little while Emily was back. "How did you do?" asked Sandy. "I suppose you won as usual."

"No," said Emily, "I came in last in my heat."

"Then why are you smiling?" asked Sandy.

"Because I did my best time—I was under 36 seconds."

Emily sat down next to Sandy. "You know," Emily said as she dried her face with a towel, "when I was seven I used to lose a lot like you. And I felt bad. Nobody *likes* to lose. Then my dad told me there are two kinds of winning. Winning against yourself and winning against others. Sometimes you can win both ways. But not often. We both did our best and lost to girls that are older and bigger and stronger than we are. We really didn't have much of a chance to beat them. We both bettered our times. If we try our hardest and we keep winning against ourselves like we did today, it won't be long before we'll be winning against others. You don't ever really lose if you win against yourself."

Sandy began to feel better, lots better. And when the loudspeaker announced her next event, a 25-yard backstroke race for eight and under girls, she got up from her towel with a big smile on her face. "Maybe I won't win in one way," she told Emily, "but if I don't, I think I'll win in another."